The Peanut Pickle

A Story about Peanut Allergy

by Jessica Ureel

illustrated by Elizabeth Brazeal

First Page Publications

12103 Merriman • Livonia, MI 48150
1-800-343-3034 • Fax (734) 525-4420
www.firstpagepublications.com

Publisher's Cataloging-in-Publication

Ureel, Jessica.
    The peanut pickle : a story about a peanut allergy / by
Jessica Ureel ; illustrated by Elizabeth Brazeal.
    p. cm.
    SUMMARY: Ben is allergic to peanuts and has to learn to
speak up about his allergy so he can have just as much fun as
everyone else and still be safe.
    ISBN 1-928623-45-X

    1. Allergy--Juvenile literature. 2. Peanuts--Health aspects--
Juvenile literature. [1. Food allergy. 2.Allergy. 3. Peanuts.]
    I. Brazeal, Elizabeth.
    II. Title.

      RC585.U74 2004   616.97
                   QBI04-700338

First Page Publications
12103 Merriman
Livonia, MI 48150
www.firstpagepublications.com

Disclaimer: The information contained herein is not intended to be a substitute
for professional medical advice. Please seek the advice of your physician with
regards to your food allergies.

For Grant and Hope

My name is Ben and I am six years old. I am like other six-year-olds in most ways, except for one thing. I can't eat peanuts or peanut butter. I can't even touch them. That's because I'm allergic to peanuts. When I was two years old, I took a bite of peanut butter and got really sick. My lips swelled up and I got hives all over me. I couldn't breathe well and had to go to the hospital.

I don't want to get sick like that again. To stay safe, I have to be very careful about what I eat. I have to ask people not to eat peanuts or peanut butter when they are with me. Sometimes it's hard to tell others about my food allergy. Sometimes I am scared to talk. That's when I take a deep breath and do it anyway. I always feel better after I speak up.

One day, my mom and I picked up my friend,
Brandon, at his house. We were going to the park.
He had a bag of snacks with him. Before we even
pulled out of the driveway, we found out what was
in the bag.

We learned the snack was, you guessed it, peanuts! I said, "Brandon, will you leave those peanuts at home? I'm allergic to them." Brandon wondered why he couldn't bring the peanuts with him so I told him that I might get sick if I touched them.

"I don't want you to get sick," he said, "I'll be right back!" He walked back to his house and handed them to his mom.

Another time, I was talking to my cousin on the phone. They were getting ready to come over and visit us that afternoon. She said they were bringing peanut butter and jelly sandwiches over to our house for lunch.

"Sarah, I am allergic to peanuts. Would you leave those peanut butter and jelly sandwiches at home?" I asked.

"Oh, yes," Sarah answered, "I am sorry, Ben. I forgot."

When they got to our house, my mom made us homemade pizza for lunch. Sarah said it was the best pizza she ever had.

Last Christmas, my Aunt Carly brought over a plate of homemade cookies. They looked delicious, but I didn't know if they were safe for me to eat. "Do any of those cookies have peanuts in them?" I asked. "If they do, they will have to stay in your car. I have a peanut allergy."

My aunt said they had no peanuts or peanut butter in them. She had remembered about my peanut allergy and wanted me to be safe. She had made my favorite butter cookies. I love my Aunt Carly!

I play on a t-ball team. It's my favorite sport.
One of my teammates brought peanut butter granola
bars to practice. He was going to share them with
the team. I knew I couldn't stay and play ball if the
other kids started eating them.

"Adam," I said, "I'm allergic to peanuts. It wouldn't be safe for me to stay at practice if everyone was eating peanut butter bars. Can you hand them out after practice, after I go home?"

"Sure, I don't mind waiting," Adam said.

We all drank lemonade during practice instead of eating a snack.

At Easter, my grandma brought over some candy for me. I like candy but I have to be careful about what kind I eat. "Are there peanuts in it?" I asked. My grandma said she didn't know. There were no ingredient labels on the candy.

"I can't eat food without an ingredient label," I told her. "My mom and dad always check the label before I eat something. Without the label, we don't know what's in the candy."

My grandma said she was sorry and that next Easter she would bring me a toy instead of candy. That sounded great to me!

At school one time, a girl in my class brought cupcakes for her birthday. When she started to hand one to me, I said, "Teresa, I can't eat those. I have a peanut allergy."

"These are chocolate, not peanut butter," she said.

"Sometimes food can have little bits of peanut in it," I told Teresa, "I can't eat food unless my mom or dad says its okay. I have a special snack for me. Mrs. Hardy is getting my treat."

My teacher kept a bag of safe snacks for me in the classroom. That way I would always have something to eat while the other kids ate their treats.

My family and I went to a pool party in the summer. When we got there, we saw bowls of peanuts sitting on all the tables. Lots of people were already there and had been eating them. It wasn't a safe place for me to be, so we had to leave. I was sad because we couldn't stay.

It looked like a fun party and I really wanted to swim. But there were just too many peanuts around there! Instead we went to a park and played at the playground. We had a picnic lunch there, too. It turned out to be a fun day after all.

One day, my neighbor and her little brother came over and asked me to play ball with them. I really wanted to play but her little brother was eating peanut butter crackers and he had sticky peanut butter all over his hands and face.

I said, "Thanks for asking, but I can't play with you right now. Your brother has peanut butter all over him and I'm allergic to it. Can you come back later when he's all cleaned up? We can play then."

"C'mon, Max," said Julia, "Let's go home and have mom wash you up. Then we can come back and play with Ben."

I go to lots of different places. If food is there, I have to ask what's in it. If someone is eating food near me, I have to find out what it is. I stay away from peanuts and peanut butter. I don't want to get sick again.

My peanut allergy is a part of me. It goes with me wherever I go. And that's okay. People who care about me want me to stay safe and healthy. I care about myself, too.

If you have a peanut allergy, remember these rules:

1. Always check food labels before eating any food.

2. Carry your Epi-Pen® with you at all times.

3. Wear your medical alert bracelet.

4. Do not eat food if you don't know what's in it.

5. If you eat something and feel sick, tell an adult right away.

Note to parents:

Peanut allergies among children are growing at an alarming rate. The reason for this increase is unclear. Approximately 1% of the U.S. population is allergic to peanuts and/or tree nuts (roughly 3 million people). It is important to remember that this is a potentially life-threatening, and usually life-long, condition. Very few children outgrow their allergy to peanuts. Prevention and planning are necessary to help prevent an accidental ingestion. Refer to the following guidelines to help decrease your child's risk of a reaction:

1. Always read food labels on everything before you allow your child to eat.

2. Have your child's Epi-Pen® and antihistamine with him/her at all times.

3. If you are not with your child, make sure a responsible adult knows the signs of an allergic reaction and how to treat it.

4. Have an emergency plan in case of accidental ingestion.

5. Teach your child not to accept food from others without your approval.

6. Do not allow your child to eat foods from bakeries or Chinese restaurants. The chance for cross-contamination is very high in these places.

7. Educate yourself on food allergies. Stay informed.

To order additional copies of this book,
please visit:

www.peanutallergykids.com

Check out our website for additional
products and information related
to peanut allergy!

Additional Resources:

foodallergy.org
The Food Allergy & Anaphylaxis Network

aanma.org
Allergy & Asthma Network, Mothers of Asthmatics

The Peanut Allergy Answer Book
(Fair Winds Press, 2001), Michael C. Young, M.D.